The Million-Dollar Bear

THE MILLION-DOLLAR BEAR

by William Kotzwinkle • illustrated by David Catrow

Alfred A. Knopf • New York

THIS IS A BORZOI BOOK PUBLISHED BY ALFRED A. KNOPF, INC.

Library of Congress Cataloging-in-Publication Data

Kotzwinkle, William.
The Million-Dollar Bear / by William Kotzwinkle ; illustrated by David Catrow.
p.   cm.
Summary: After escaping from the vault in a millionaire's home, a very valuable old teddy bear
finds happiness with a family who knows his true worth.
ISBN 0-679-85295-6 (trade) — ISBN 0-679-95295-0 (lib. bdg.)
[1. Teddy bears—Fiction.] I. Catrow, David, ill. II. Title.
PZ7.K855Mi   1995   93-6262
[E]—dc20

Manufactured in Singapore
10 9 8 7 6 5 4 3 2 1

For all bears everywhere
—W. K.

For Deb, who likes me just the way I am
—D. C.

Argyle Oldhouse was a grouchy old millionaire. The only things he loved in this world were teddy bears. He had hundreds of them, worth a fortune. "You bears are priceless," he'd say to them every day, and they'd look back at him from their little chairs.

"You're good bears, and you're *my* bears." Argyle Oldhouse gave them each a pat on the head as he walked by. "These are the best bears in the world," he said to himself. "And they're all mine. I don't have to share them with anybody."

Argyle Oldhouse marched along through his mansion. "Everywhere you look, you see bears, and that's the way I like it."

When bedtime came, he had the butler say good night to all the bears. "If you miss one of them, you're fired."

"Very good, sir," said the butler. Then he said good night to the bears.

"And *I'll* say good night to the Million-Dollar Bear." Argyle Oldhouse opened a vault in the wall. "Any bear worth a million dollars is going to get Argyle Oldhouse's own personal good night."

The Million-Dollar Bear's button eyes squinted when the lights came on in the vault. He wasn't allowed out, ever, because he was too valuable.

"What a bear." Argyle Oldhouse stared at the Million-Dollar Bear. "You look like a million dollars tonight. You look like a million dollars every night. You're my kind of bear."

The Million-Dollar Bear didn't feel like a million dollars. He just felt like a bear. But because he was so valuable, he didn't get to visit with the other bears. He just stayed in the vault all day, in the dark.

"I can't take chances," said Argyle Oldhouse. "Not with a Million-Dollar Bear."

The Million-Dollar Bear pleaded with his little button eyes.

"What a wonderful expression," said Argyle Oldhouse. "It's worth a million dollars."

The Million-Dollar Bear didn't know why he was so valuable. His head was a little threadbare, and his label was long gone.

"You're the genuine article," said Argyle Oldhouse. "The antique, one and only, original Teddy Bear. And you're mine. Nobody sees you but me. What do you think of that?"

I'm so lonely, thought the Million-Dollar Bear, and he began to cry.

"What a bear," said Argyle Oldhouse as he closed the vault. Then he went to bed with two dozen bears.

"You're good bears," he said, and pulled up the covers. Then he fell asleep.

When he awoke in the morning, he was surrounded by bears. "That's the way I like it," he said, and he gave each of the bears a quarter. Which they couldn't spend. So he kept the quarters for them.

Then he walked through his mansion, straight to the vault. The vault was open, and the Million-Dollar Bear was gone.

"Vanished!" cried Argyle Oldhouse. "There's only one person who could have done this."

Argyle Oldhouse sent for his car. "Take me to the residence of J. P. Plumpgarden."

He arrived at the mansion of J. P. Plumpgarden and demanded to see him at once. "It's about a bear," said Argyle Oldhouse. "He'll understand."

J. P. Plumpgarden appeared. "Well, well, what can I do for you, Oldhouse?"

"You've stolen my bear, Plumpgarden."

"That's correct."

"You admit it?"

"Certainly. I never lie."

"I'll have you thrown in jail!"

"You'll have to prove I stole your bear," said J. P. Plumpgarden. "And that you shall never do. Now, if you'll excuse me, I must say good morning to my bears."

J. P. Plumpgarden's house was filled with bears. He walked along, shaking their paws and bowing to the more important ones.

Argyle Oldhouse left angrily. "No one can steal my Million-Dollar Bear and get away with it," he thundered.

J. P. Plumpgarden laughed as he watched Argyle Oldhouse ride away. "All's fair in love and bears," he said, and went straight to *his* vault, where the Million-Dollar Bear was locked in the dark. Again.

Please, said the Million-Dollar Bear, *don't keep me in the vault.*

"You'll be glad to know I had this vault made especially in your honor," said J. P. Plumpgarden. "The temperature is perfect for a stuffed animal."

But it's dark, said the Million-Dollar Bear.

"And it's waterproof, bulletproof, and burglarproof."

But it's lonely, said the Million-Dollar Bear.

J. P. Plumpgarden closed the vault.

The Million-Dollar Bear sat in the dark. *I wish I wasn't worth a million dollars,* he said to himself.

But he was. He was the most valuable bear in the world.

At twelve noon the vault opened and the butler said, "Lunch is served, sir."

The Million-Dollar Bear's button eyes opened wide. *Will I be allowed to visit with the other bears?*

"You sit at one end of the table, and I sit at the other," said J. P. Plumpgarden. The table was so long the Million-Dollar Bear could hardly see J. P. Plumpgarden. *But it's better than being in the vault,* said the Million-Dollar Bear.

"I like to have lunch with a valuable bear," said J. P. Plumpgarden. "It improves my appetite. And afterward I take a nap."

He took a nap, right in his chair. The butler didn't know what to do with the Million-Dollar Bear. He was afraid to move him. So he left him sitting there.

The Million-Dollar Bear looked around. *So this is what a house looks like,* he said to himself. *I'd almost forgotten.*

Long ago, so long ago he could hardly remember, he'd belonged to a little girl who had played with him every day. *I wasn't valuable back then,* said the Million-Dollar Bear. *I was worth about a dollar and a half. Those were the days.*

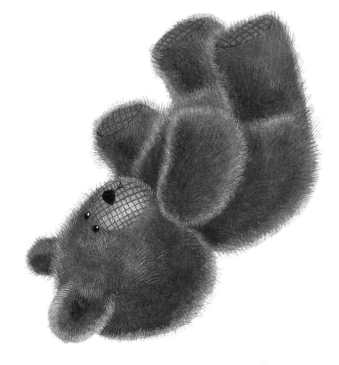

J. P. Plumpgarden snored on. He didn't hear the doorbell.

"Squeegee Cleaning Company," said the man at the door. "I'm C. G. Squeegee."

"You're to clean the chairs," said the butler.

"Right." C. G. Squeegee thought the butler said "Clean the bears." He put all the bears in his truck and drove off. "Quite a load of bears," he said to himself.

There's been a mistake, said the Panda Bear. *He was supposed to clean the* CHAIRS, *not the* BEARS.

Who cares? cried the Million-Dollar Bear. *I'm out of the vault! I'm talking to another bear.*

Rare, is it? asked the Koala Bear.

It's so rare I can't remember when I last talked to another bear, said the Million-Dollar Bear.

Why are you so valuable? asked the Little Brown Bear.

I don't know, said the Million-Dollar Bear. *I just am.*

He was the first Teddy Bear ever made, said the Black Bear. *That's why he's worth a million dollars.*

The other bears nodded respectfully and grew silent. They just stared at the Million-Dollar Bear.

Please, said the Million-Dollar Bear, *I'm just like the rest of you.*

No, said the Black Bear, *you're the original.*

The truck hit a big bump. The back door flew open. C. G. Squeegee looked in his rearview mirror. "Why, a bunch of bears just fell out."

He parked his truck. "Bears everywhere," said C. G. Squeegee. There were bears in the bushes and bears in the mud. There were bears at the bottom of some cellar stairs.

"Sorry about that," said C. G. Squeegee, and he put them back in the truck.

Stop! cried the Panda Bear. *We've lost the Million-Dollar Bear!*

"They're a nice quiet bunch of bears," said C. G. Squeegee, and he drove away.

The Million-Dollar Bear lay on a pile of trash bags. Only his ear was sticking out. It looked like a soggy doughnut. Nobody noticed him at all.

I'm out in the world at last, said the Million-Dollar Bear. He'd gotten a tear in his tummy, but he didn't care. He was happier in the trash bags than he'd ever been in his temperature-controlled, waterproof, bullet-proof, burglarproof vault.

The afternoon went by, and he listened to the sounds of the world with his one ear that looked like a soggy doughnut.

I'm hearing it all now, he said.

Meanwhile, J. P. Plumpgarden had finished his nap. "Where's the Million-Dollar Bear?" he asked his butler.

"I fear I've made a terrible mistake, sir. He's being cleaned."

"Cleaned? Are you crazy? You don't clean a Million-Dollar Bear!" J. P. Plumpgarden looked around the empty room. "Where are the other bears?"

"They're being cleaned too, sir," said the butler.

J. P. Plumpgarden got red in the face. "Get out!" he shouted. "You're fired!"

"Very good, sir," said the butler, who'd been fired by J. P. Plumpgarden five hundred times before.

"Come back here," said J. P. Plumpgarden. "*Who* is cleaning the bears?"

"A Mr. C. G. Squeegee, sir, of the Squeegee Cleaning Company."

"It could have been Argyle Oldhouse in disguise, here to steal my Million-Dollar Bear."

"He did not resemble Mr. Oldhouse in any way, sir."

"That remains to be seen," said J. P. Plumpgarden. "Send for my car."

"Am I to understand, sir, that I am once again in your employ?"

"Yes, certainly. Don't ask silly questions."

"Very good, sir."

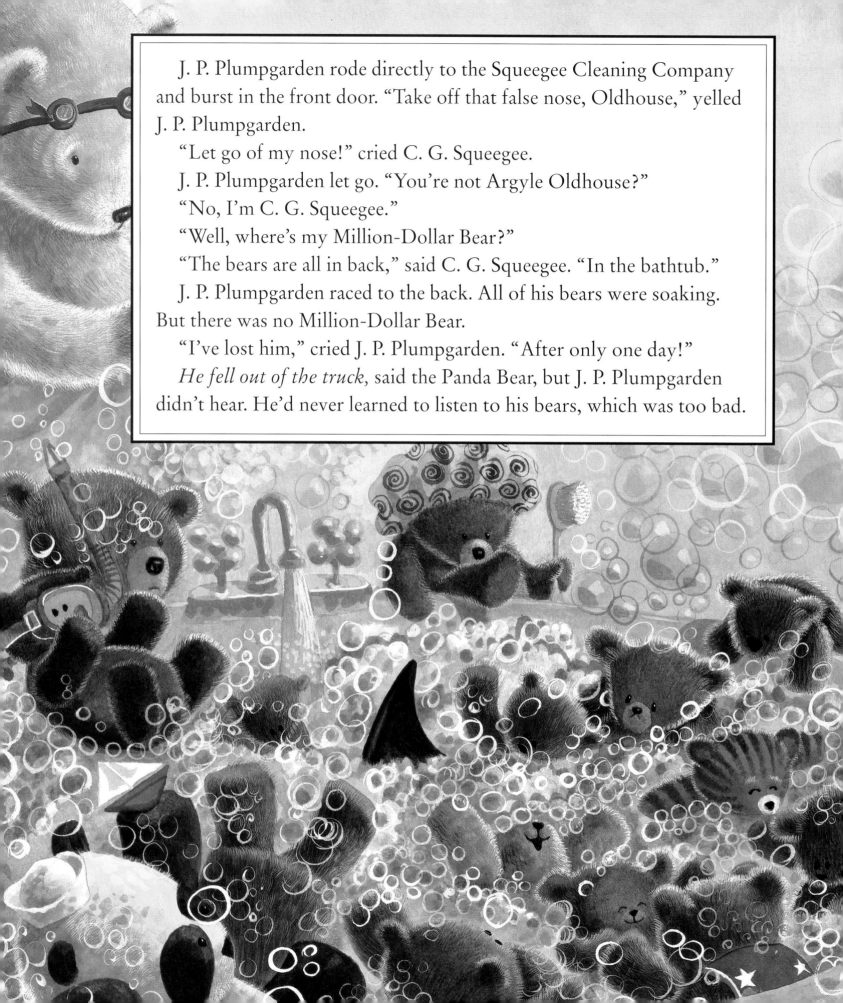

J. P. Plumpgarden rode directly to the Squeegee Cleaning Company and burst in the front door. "Take off that false nose, Oldhouse," yelled J. P. Plumpgarden.

"Let go of my nose!" cried C. G. Squeegee.

J. P. Plumpgarden let go. "You're not Argyle Oldhouse?"

"No, I'm C. G. Squeegee."

"Well, where's my Million-Dollar Bear?"

"The bears are all in back," said C. G. Squeegee. "In the bathtub."

J. P. Plumpgarden raced to the back. All of his bears were soaking. But there was no Million-Dollar Bear.

"I've lost him," cried J. P. Plumpgarden. "After only one day!"

He fell out of the truck, said the Panda Bear, but J. P. Plumpgarden didn't hear. He'd never learned to listen to his bears, which was too bad.

Back at the trash bags, the Million-Dollar Bear was having a splendid time, listening to people walking by. He only heard a few words here and there, but he didn't care. *I'm part of the world,* he said to himself. *I belong!*

Just then a boy named Biff Bang came by, pulling his red wagon. When he saw an ear sticking out of the trash bags, he knew it wasn't a soggy doughnut. "That's a bear," said Biff Bang.

It certainly is, said the Million-Dollar Bear.

Biff Bang lifted the Million-Dollar Bear out of the trash bags. The Million-Dollar Bear got a view of the whole street. *How beautiful the world is,* he said.

"You're pretty old," said Biff Bang. "Is that why they threw you in the trash?" He looked the Million-Dollar Bear over carefully. "I'm going to take you home with me."

You don't have a vault there, do you? asked the Million-Dollar Bear.

Biff Bang sat the Million-Dollar Bear in the back of his red wagon.

The Million-Dollar Bear saw the sky and the trees. He saw the houses and the yards. He saw people walking. It was very exciting, but he was still worried about vaults. He tried to lean forward and explain about vaults to Biff. *A vault,* he said, *is a dark room with a lock on it. And bears don't do well in them. You don't have one of those, do you?*

"Hang on," said Biff Bang, and he pulled the wagon as fast as he could.

The Million-Dollar Bear bounced up and down. His button eyes sparkled with excitement. *I'm watching the world roll by,* he said.

Meanwhile, Argyle Oldhouse was putting on a red wig and beard and a false nose. He stuffed a pillow in his shirt.

"Now *that's* a disguise," he said to himself. "No one could possibly see through it."

He stepped outside his mansion. A little girl who was walking along with her mother said, "Mommy, that man is wearing a false nose!"

"Shhhhh," said her mother. "You mustn't talk about the poor man's nose that way."

"But it's not *real!*" insisted the girl, and her mother had to yank her along by the arm.

"A moderately effective disguise," said Argyle Oldhouse. "But it's enough to fool J. P. Plumpgarden, because Plumpgarden hasn't got a brain in his head."

He went to J. P. Plumpgarden's mansion and rang the bell.

"Yes?" asked the butler.

"I'm from *Rare Bear* magazine," said Argyle Oldhouse. "I'd like to photograph your collection."

"Please step this way," said the butler.

The bears had all been cleaned by C. G. Squeegee and were back in their chairs. Argyle Oldhouse pretended to photograph them. "*Rare Bear* magazine has recently learned that your employer now owns the Million-Dollar Bear."

"I am not at liberty to discuss that," said the butler.

Just then, J. P. Plumpgarden entered. "Oldhouse!" he cried. "Take off that ridiculous disguise!"

"I beg your pardon," said Argyle Oldhouse. "I'm from *Rare Bear* magazine."

"You're wearing a false nose," said J. P. Plumpgarden, and he pulled it off. And threw it on the floor. And stepped on it.

"How dare you step on my nose!" cried Argyle Oldhouse.

"Oh, be quiet," said J. P. Plumpgarden. "And if you're here to try and steal back the Million-Dollar Bear, you're wasting your time. He's disappeared."

"What?" Stunned, Argyle Oldhouse removed his false beard.

"Yes, he was sent out to be cleaned. And the cleaning man lost him."

"You sent the Million-Dollar Bear out to be cleaned?"

"I didn't. *He* did." J. P. Plumpgarden pointed to his butler.

"Is this true?" asked Argyle Oldhouse.

"Yes," said the butler.

"You're fired!" shouted Argyle Oldhouse.

"Just a minute, Oldhouse," said J. P. Plumpgarden. "I won't have you firing my butler."

"Oh, shut up," said Argyle Oldhouse.

The two old millionaires looked at each other. They were a sorry sight. Their hearts were broken. Their Million-Dollar Bear was gone. They started to cry.

"It's at a time like this that a man should share his bears," said J. P. Plumpgarden. And he had the butler carry all the bears into the living room. Then J. P. Plumpgarden and Argyle Oldhouse got down on the carpet and covered themselves in bears. It made both of them feel much better, and the bears liked it too.

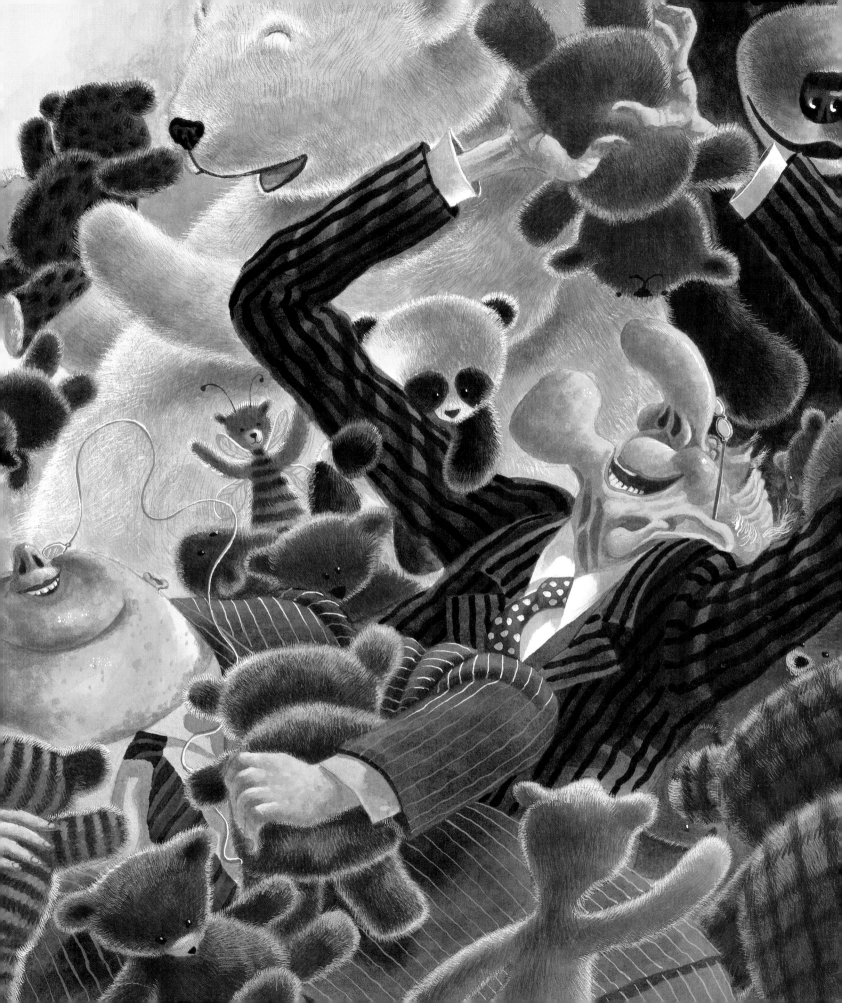

Meanwhile, Biff Bang and the Million-Dollar Bear had arrived at a run-down little house. "This is where I live," said Biff.

Just so long as you don't have a vault, said the Million-Dollar Bear.

Biff carried the Million-Dollar Bear into the house.

"Well, who's this?" asked Biff's mother when she saw the Million-Dollar Bear.

"I found him in the trash," said Biff.

The Million-Dollar Bear looked around, his button eyes glowing with curiosity. There was a dog under the stove. There was a cat looking out of a grocery bag. There was a parrot in a cage, breaking peanuts with his beak. And there was an elderly gentleman in a rocking chair.

"Bring that bear over here," said the elderly gentleman.

"Meet Grandfather," said Biff.

"This bear has seen a lot of territory," said Grandfather as he took the Million-Dollar Bear in his lap. "Reminds me of the bear I used to have. I used to keep him—"

In a vault? asked the Million-Dollar Bear.

"—in my bed," said Grandfather. "We watched the moon come over the trees every night. He was a deep thinker, that bear of mine. This bear appears to be a deep thinker too."

Somebody's crying, said the Million-Dollar Bear.

"Biff," said Mother, "go see to Fanny."

You don't keep her in a vault, do you? asked the Million-Dollar Bear.

Grandfather stood the Million-Dollar Bear on his knees. He bounced the Million-Dollar Bear up and down. "They don't make bears the way they used to," said Grandfather.

Biff brought Fanny out in his arms. "See the bear, Fanny?"

"Bear," said Fanny.

How do you do, said the Million-Dollar Bear.

"She stopped crying," said Biff.

Biff's father came home from work. "I see we've acquired a bear," he said.

"All right, everybody," said Mother. "It's time for supper."

The Million-Dollar Bear was put in the high chair with Fanny. She petted him and kissed him, but he couldn't enjoy it because the subject of vaults had not been cleared up. Was he going to be put in one? That was the question. If he was, he'd have to make another daring escape.

"Bear," said Fanny. She fed him from her bowl and got him all smutched up with food.

"Look what Fanny's doing to your bear," said Mother to Biff.

"He's her bear now," said Biff.

The table was crowded. There was Mother, Father, Biff, and Fanny. There was Grandfather. And there was Uncle Bob, who lived in the back room. Uncle Bob was a tailor. He said he'd sew up the tear in the Million-Dollar Bear. "He'll look just like new," said Uncle Bob.

"That bear will never look new," said Grandfather. "He's as old as I am."

"Does that mean he's valuable?" asked Biff.

"He's not worth a red cent," said Grandfather.

When bedtime came, the Million-Dollar Bear got very nervous. Bedtime was vault time.

"Bear," said Fanny, holding out her arms.

"The bear stays with me," said Grandfather. "For safekeeping."

Oh no, said the Million-Dollar Bear. *He's going to put me in a safe.*

Everybody went to bed except Grandfather and the Million-Dollar Bear. Grandfather sat in his rocking chair and looked at the Million-Dollar Bear for a long time. "I used to tell my bear things I couldn't tell anyone else. When I was frightened, or ashamed, I'd talk to him. He never said a word, but I knew he understood. When I got blamed for things that weren't my fault, I'd tell him, and I'd feel better. Sometimes, if I was angry, I'd give him a punch. He never complained. He knew I didn't mean it. He was the best friend I ever had."

Grandfather's eyes seemed like two watery buttons. A tear ran down his cheek. "It's good to have a bear around the house again." He stood up. "Well, time to put you where you'll be safe."

Here it comes, groaned the Million-Dollar Bear.

Grandfather carried the Million-Dollar Bear to Fanny's room and laid him in bed with her.

Fanny put her arms around him and said "Bear," very softly, in her sleep.

The Million-Dollar Bear lay in her arms. He could see the moon coming over the trees. He could hear the sounds of the sleeping world. He could feel Fanny's tiny hand on his cheek. *I'm the happiest bear on earth*, said the Million-Dollar Bear.

Why is that? asked the moon.

Because I'm not worth a red cent, said the Million-Dollar Bear.